If the S in MOOSE Comes Loose

Story by PETER HERMANN   Pictures by MATTHEW CORDELL

HARPER

An Imprint of HarperCollinsPublishers

ISBN 978-0-06-229510-1

The artist used pen and ink with watercolor to create the illustrations for this book.

Typography by Rachel Zegar

18   19   20   21   SCP   10   9   8   7   6   5   4   3   2

❖

First Edition

For my A's: August, Amaya, and Andrew—
and of course my M . . .
—P.H.

To Eva Esrum, my high school art teacher.
Thank you for giving so much.
—M.C.

If the S in MOOSE comes loose and the E breaks free... what's left?

A gloomy **MOO** from **COW**, who doesn't know what to do,
all alone without her **MOOSE**,
whose **E** broke free and whose **S** came loose.

But COW has an idea!

"I'll get some **GLUE!**"

"Then I'll **MOO** my best **MOO** and slather the **GLUE**
all over the **S** and on the **E**, too.
I'll press my **MOO** and those letters together,
and my **MOOSE** will be back, better than ever!"

"I gather you know you begin with a **G**.

Could I get you to graciously give it to me?"

GOAT scratches his beard.

"Sounds weird. What'll I be without my **G**?"

"What'll you be!?" says **COW**. "Wait here and see!"

COW bolts to find her buddy **BEAR**,
asleep, as usual, in his favorite chair.

"Hope you don't mind if I borrow your **B**.
I've got a **MOOSE** emergency.
Your fur and claws will disappear, and you'll be, well—"

"I got it, GOAT! This B for your G ...and ahoy!"

"You're a BOAT!"

"And me? I get a **G** for my GLUE!
First letter's done, now where's letter two?
I'll glue my **MOOSE**, if it's the last thing I do!"

COW races for the **C** in CHAIR.

"I hope you'll be comfortable sitting on **HAIR**!"

"I'll put this C where the L used to be...."

And instead of the LAKE, BOAT's sailing on CAKE!

"**G** is done. **L** is, too!

I'll glue my **MOOSE**, if it's the last thing I do."

"Now, where in the world

would I get a—"

"GOAT is gone; a BOAT's on a CAKE.
It also looks like we've lost our LAKE.
BEAR has vanished into thin air.
And what's with the EAR on that heap of HAIR?"

"It's like this," sputters COW. "My MOOSE came undone.
I'm making GLUE and—oh, BULL! I never knew!
You've got the most enchanting U!"

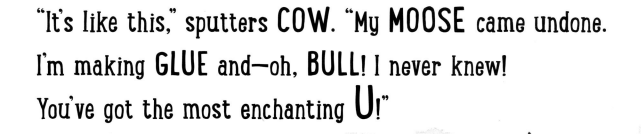

"Enchanting?" BULL blushes. Could it be true?

"It's yours," says BULL, "if it's useful to—"

COW's on the run, but there's nowhere to hide.
Wait! A **HOUSE**!
She ducks inside!

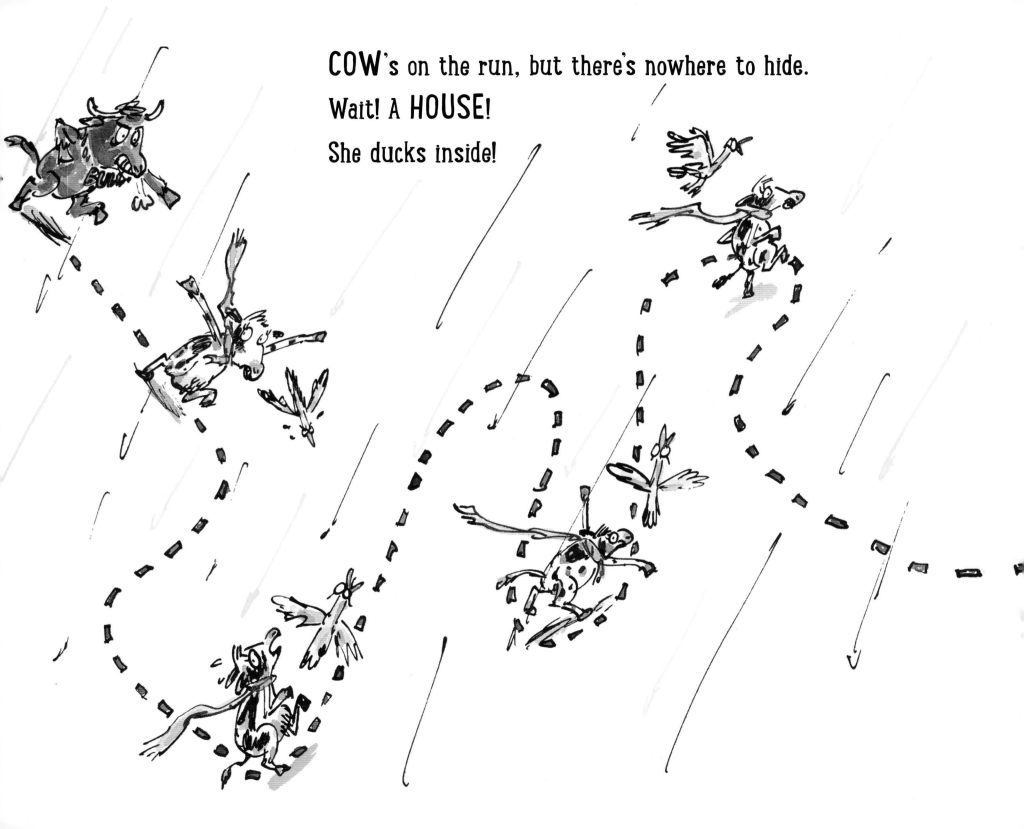

HOUSE has a **U** right there in the middle!
COW pulls and pushes and tugs it a little,
and **HOUSE** with no **U** leaves...

...a HOSE!

COW wants her MOOSE back! Anything goes!

"Listen, EAR, you began as a BEAR, I dismantled your CHAIR—
I need your E! Last thing, I swear."
EAR eyes COW uneasily.

"Oh no! **BULL**'s still after me!"

Off in a flash,
COW makes a mad dash.
Wait! A CART! Look out—

COW grabs the C that came off the CART!
(And BULL's left behind with some very strange ART.)

"Look, Ear! A C! Here you are!"

"...which finally completes my GLUE!
I'm ready, MOOSE, to reglue you!
I'll—just—M-O-O—"

"HOLD IT!

M-O-O-?

Where is the S?

Where is the E?

Without them, my MOO is useless to me."

COW jumps in the CAR and grabs the wheel!
The engine roars, the tires squeal!
She scoops up the S, right where it fell,
and chases down the E as well.

She slams on the brakes, she leaps out the door—
this is the moment she's waited for!

COW stirs her GLUE...

takes a deep breath, too...

and MOOs the best MOO she can possibly do.

She GLUEs the S right next to the O
and sticks the E on the end just so.
And then . . .

"Welcome back, my beloved friend."

"Thank you," says MOOSE,
"for putting me—and us—together again."